Postman Pat® and the
Surprise Present

SIMON AND SCHUSTER

Pat was on his rounds when he spotted Dr Gilbertson walking along the road.

"Hello, Dr Gilbertson!" he called. "What are you doing so far from home?"

"Hello, Pat. I'm on my way to see Alf. He's in bed with a bad cold."

"Hop in, then!" said Pat. "Jess and I are going that way."

"It must be hard work visiting patients without a car," said Pat.

"Oh, I can't complain," said Dr Gilbertson. "Home visits are all part of my job, Pat – but it's nice to have a lift!"

When they arrived at Thompson Ground, Pat handed Dr Gilbertson a letter. "This is for you!"

"Oh! A birthday card from my sister."

"Is it your birthday soon?" asked Pat.

"It's today, Pat - but I'm far too busy for birthdays. Thanks for the lift!"

Julian and Charlie were walking Bonnie, when they bumped into Sarah Gilbertson. She looked very gloomy.

"What's the matter, Sarah?" Julian asked.

"It's Mum's birthday today, and I can't think what to get her. It's got to be really special."

"I've got an idea!" smiled Charlie. "But first, we need Lucy. Follow me!"

Pat dropped in at Ted's, and told him about Dr Gilbertson.
"Visiting all her patients on foot? We've got to do summat," muttered
Ted, rummaging through a pile of rubbish. "How about a skateboard –
or roller skates?"
"I think what Dr Gilbertson really needs is a car," said Pat.
"A car, eh? Come and look at this, Pat."

"What d'you reckon?" asked Ted, lifting the tarpaulin off an old car.

"She's a beauty," gasped Pat.

"You're right there, Pat. There's just one problem – she hasn't started in years."

Ted tried the engine. It coughed and spluttered.

"Aye aye, what's going on here, then?" asked PC Selby, who'd heard all the spluttering.

"It's Dr Gilbertson's birthday today," Pat told him, "and we want to fix up the car as a present."

"Trouble is, she won't start," sighed Ted.

"Hmm – what you need is an expert," said PC Selby.

"Like Ajay!" smiled Pat. "Let's give him a call."

At the cafe, Ajay told Nisha, Sara and the vicar all about Pat and Ted's plan. "Let's organise a surprise tea party!" suggested Nisha.

The children were in the schoolhouse, getting their own surprise
ready – a special birthday song!

"Right," said Charlie. "We've got our keyboard, our drummer, and
our singers. Let's get to it!"

Sarah wasn't very good at singing in tune – and neither was Bonnie! "Woof! Woof! Aooooo!"

"D'you know what, Bonnie," Sarah smiled.

"I think we'd better leave the singing to the people who are good at it."

Bonnie gave her a big lick on the cheek.

Ajay arrived at Ted's, and had a good look at the car.

"Well, it's nothing I can't fix," he said, "with the right tools, some spare parts, and lots of tea and biscuits! Pass me the wrench, Pat!"

"I'll give her a good clean-up," said Ted, fetching a bucket of soapy water. But he tripped over Jess, who was peering into the exhaust pipe. Jess and PC Selby got a good soaking!

In no time at all, the car was gleaming, and Ajay had fixed the engine.

"Phew, that's it, lads," he said. "Start her up, Ted!"

The car revved – then backfired, shooting a puff of smoke out of the exhaust at poor Jess!

"Oh dear!" they groaned.

Ajay had another look under the bonnet.

"It's no good, Ted. I just can't find anything wrong."

"Hold on a minute," said Pat. "I think Jess has found something."

PC Selby shone a torch into the exhaust pipe, and pulled out an old mouse nest!

"Here's your problem, Ajay!" he announced.

"No wonder Jess was so interested," grinned Pat.

Ajay climbed back into the driver's seat and started the engine again.

This time, the car purred like a tiger.

"Bingo!" cheered Ajay.

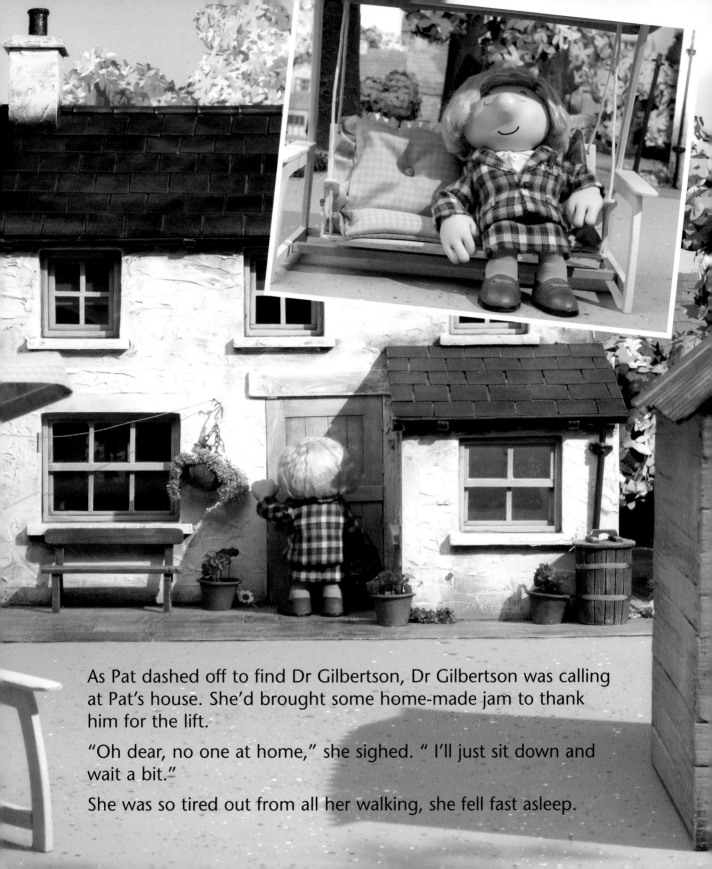

As Pat dashed off to find Dr Gilbertson, Dr Gilbertson was calling at Pat's house. She'd brought some home-made jam to thank him for the lift.

"Oh dear, no one at home," she sighed. " I'll just sit down and wait a bit."

She was so tired out from all her walking, she fell fast asleep.

On the village green, the birthday tea was all ready.

"Hello, Pat," called Sara. "What do you think?"

"It looks grand, Sara," said Pat. "But now I can't find Dr Gilbertson."

Jess knew exactly where she was!

"Goodness me, Jess," yawned Dr Gilbertson, "I'd better get home!"

On her way past the green, Dr Gilbertson spotted the tea all laid out.

"Gosh, it must be some sort of special occasion."

"Miaow!" said Jess.

PC Selby suddenly zoomed up on his bike.

"Halt!" he commanded. "Stay where you are, please, doctor. Police orders!" He blew his whistle. . .

. . . and out of nowhere, all the villagers appeared, carrying presents and flowers for Dr Gilbertson.

The children performed their birthday song – even Sarah and Bonnie joined in!

"Oh thank you, children, that was marvellous!" beamed Dr Gilbertson.

Sarah gave her mother a big hug.

Just then, there was a loud horn blast, and Ted and Ajay drove up.

"Oh, what a lovely car," admired Dr Gilbertson.

"Do you like it, Doctor?" asked Ted.

"Oh yes, it's beautiful!"

"Well that's good," said Ajay. "Because it's for you!"

Dr Gilbertson was lost for words. She just smiled and smiled.

"And this is from me," said PC Selby. "It's a tool kit – in case the car ever breaks down."

"Oh Arthur, how kind!" beamed Dr Gilbertson, giving him a kiss.

"Pat, everybody, I don't know what to say!"

"There's nothing to say," laughed Pat, "except . . . Happy Birthday , Dr Gilbertson!"

SIMON AND SCHUSTER
First published in 2007 in Great Britain by Simon & Schuster UK Ltd
Africa House, 64-78 Kingsway
London WC2B 6AH
A CBS COMPANY

This hardback edition published in 2007

A CIP catalogue record for this book is available from the British Library upon request

ISBN-10: 1-84738-072-7
ISBN-13: 978-1-84738-072-2

Printed in China
1 3 5 7 9 10 8 6 4 2